A Romance to Freedom & Pride

BY

Eidahs

EDITED BY JONATHON SAWYER & BINKY INK

COVER BY BINKY INK

BINKY INK
THE LITERARY ARM OF BINKY PRODUCTIONS

WWW.BINKYPRODUCTIONS.COM/SHORTSTORIES

<u>WARNINGS:</u>

Homophobia, violence.

Table of Contents

<u>A ROMANCE TO FREEDOM AND PRIDE</u>

Present Day — July 20th, 2005. Canada.

Aidan waltzed out onto the porch where sat Markus, and thrust the newspaper he was carrying in his face.

'We can finally get married!'

Markus chuckled, looking up at Aidan. 'In our forties?'

Aidan placed himself in front of Markus, leaning his hands on the other's knees. 'Markus, I've been wanting to marry you since I was eighteen.'

Markus smiled warmly. 'So have I.'

* * *

26 Years Earlier — All Boys Boarding School,
October 1979.

From the library window, Aidan watched the other lads as they scurried through the school's terrain, scaled the fence at the other end, and jumped to the other side for a not-so-clandestine rendezvous with the girls from the neighbouring boarding school. The rule was 'No dating allowed.'

'They are *so* going to get in trouble,' he muttered to himself.

Chuckling brought his attention to the lad leaning against the bookshelf. 'And we are the studious ones, I presume?'

Markus always had an air about him of arrogance and pride, his uniform had not a single crease in it – he was from one of the richer families here. Aidan was quieter, kept to himself, yet often found Markus observing him. In the short time Aidan had been here, he'd found himself drawn to Markus somehow but never thought much more of it.

'It's strange that you're here only for your senior year,' said Markus, 'but I'm glad of it, regardless of the hows and whys. And I reckon I know exactly why you're not out there with the other lads.'

'Oh?' Aidan raised an eyebrow, curious. 'In the last month since the school year began, you've figured me out, have you?'

Markus pushed away from the bookshelf and came to stand very close to Aidan, his cheek nearly touching his as he leaned towards his ear, his whisper making Aidan's heart pound.

'The same reason as me. You don't like girls. Neither do I, and...' Markus pulled away just enough to stare into Aidan's eyes. 'I like you.'

His face twitched nervously, but his eyes never left Aidan's gaze. Aidan drew in a breath and realised he was smiling.

Markus backed away and offered Aidan his hand. 'Come, let's go…study in the dorm room.'

Heart racing with excitement, Aidan took Markus's hand, and the two lads nearly ran all the way to the dorms. Markus shut the door quickly, pressing Aidan against it, his lips coming very close to the other lad's. Markus's dark hair contrasted Aidan's blond head of hair, his captivating grey eyes boring deep into Aidan's brown eyes.

Markus swallowed, and murmured, 'Now, I've never actually kissed anyone before.'

'Good, because neither have I,' admitted Aidan.

Markus's smile was enticing and he bit his lower lip. 'I'd very much like to kiss you, Aidan.'

If Aidan's heart exploded right this moment, he'd die happy. He was filled with a joy he'd never before experienced and it felt so wonderful to finally know what it was he was feeling, what it was he had been feeling for Markus since his first day here.

'I'd like to kiss you too,' he whispered.

Markus leaned forward even closer and Aidan met him half-way. They kissed, tentatively pressing their lips together, then opening their mouths for more. The second kiss was sloppy and wet, the third more elating, and then their tongues twined, and they both sucked in their breaths as the kisses deepened.

Wrapping their arms around each other, they devoured each other, every kiss better than the last, every kiss leaving Aidan needing more, every kiss filling Aidan with elated relief.

Markus pulled away and led Aidan to the bed. 'We should probably get *some* studying done.'

Aidan felt like he'd been running a marathon. He laughed and joined Markus on the bed, both lying on their stomachs, books open. They studied, but kept kissing between math problems, exploring each other's mouths and feeling each other as they solved algebra equations and corrected grammar.

* * *

One month later.

Markus took Aidan by the hand and pulled him into a dark alcove, pressing him against the wall and capturing his lips in a long-needed kiss. The hall was empty but he wasn't going to take any chances.

'We're going to be late for class,' protested Aidan, just before pulling Markus back to him by the collar and engulfing his lips into his mouth, suckling the other lad's lower lip.

Markus groaned. 'You have no idea how good it feels to kiss you, Aidan. Two whole hours is way too long for me to go without you.'

'This, after a month of us sneaking around like this? How are you going to be after a year?'

The relief Markus felt at the prospect and from kissing his secret boyfriend made him burst inside.

'You see us together in a year?' he smiled, hopeful.

Aidan opened his mouth, looking shocked, as though just realising the implications of what he had said. 'Well... I guess, yeah.'

Markus bit his lower lip, feeling his face twitch. 'Of all the lads and men I've had my eye on, you're the one I approached and I...am so happy to hear you say that. Aidan, I hope we can be together in a year too. I...hope we can become more...official.'

'Secretly official?' Aidan chuckled.

Markus nodded before kissing his boyfriend again, squeezing his cheeks between his hands as he tried to get the lad's entire head in his mouth. 'I could eat you all up.'

They both chuckled.

Quickened heels alerted them of an approaching teacher. Markus fixed up Aidan's collar and uncreased his own uniform. They stepped out of the alcove, hurrying towards class.

'No running, lads!'

Markus turned around to look at the kind face of their drama teacher – she was a woman in her thirties. 'Yes, Miss Mariane.' He suppressed a laugh.

'Honestly, the times I've caught you two skulking around, one wonders what you boys are up to sometimes.'

'How's your sister?' asked Markus. He added to Aidan, 'Mariane lives with her sister.'

'She's doing just fine; thank you, Markus. Now behave and don't run.'

'Yes, Miss Mariane. By the way, your hair is just lovely today. You look radiant.'

'Flattery won't get you out of trouble, Markus. Don't make me mark you down as unruly.' She pointed to his head.

Aidan snorted in his throat as Markus put a hand to his hair and started fixing it up.

'You two, Aidan. Honestly, if you're going to tussle and wrestle, do so *after* classes are dismissed.'

'Yes, Miss Mariane.' They both replied, suppressing laughter. Markus felt himself blush, his face felt hot, and he was thinking about last night again, about their 'tussle.'

* * *

'Everyone's gone on a not-so-secret date again,' said Markus, 'which leaves the dorm completely empty for us.'

'It does.' Aidan was lying on his bed, hands clasped behind his head. He opened up his arms and Markus plopped down on top of Aidan.

'Oof,' laughed Aidan.

Markus felt nervous when he kissed Aidan, feeling something bloom inside his pelvis and he let out a sweet moan.

'Aidan,' he began, trembling, his face twitching nervously, 'I'd like to do more than just kiss tonight.'

Aidan drew in a breath and his face reddened. 'You want to have sex?'

'Yes.'

Markus had waited for Aidan to turn eighteen too, so that they could be intimate as men. They were both virgins, and Markus was determined he knew what he felt for Aidan. 'I want to be sexually intimate with you.'

'Markus, I've been wanting to be intimate with you for weeks.'

Markus let out a relieved sigh that was quickly replaced by anticipatory heavy breathing as he and Aidan kissed. This time their deep kisses led to the physical elation Markus had been craving from his boyfriend.

* * *

As soon as Mariane was out of view and the two turned the corner, Markus's lips were back on Aidan's, hungry as ever.

'Last night was amazing, by the way,' he said as he pulled away, looking around to make sure the hall was still empty.

'I wish we could get up to that again now,' admitted Aidan.

Markus's heart swelled. 'Tonight. Meet me outside by the willow tree.'

'It's a date, my secret-yet-official boyfriend.'

The two giggled boyishly and Markus capered as they ran to class, barely making it in time.

Aidan kept sending Markus flirtatious glances the whole time they were in class, it made the wait to the night agonising. But they met up that night, and it was just as amazing as the first time.

Markus had to clamp his hand over Aidan's mouth to keep him from screaming...and Aidan had to do the same to him to keep Markus from screaming.

Markus definitely knew what he felt for Aidan. And the two continued to sneak off together, steal kisses in the hallways, cuddle in the dorms when they were alone together, and pretend they were studying, all so they could spend time together as secret-yet-official boyfriends.

* * *

Several months later — April 1980.

Aidan was feeling all sorts inside his body and in his heart as he made out with Markus in the dark secluded alcove outside, leaning on his boyfriend. This had been one of their spots.

Sweat still dripped down Aidan's face as he rubbed himself up on Markus after they had redressed.

'Nothing beats being naked in the snow,' laughed Markus.

Aidan chuckled, pressing Markus against the wall and cupping his face in his hands. 'Not much snow left, though.'

'School's nearly done now, we'll be graduating in a couple of months, and then we can be together, not so much in secret.'

'People won't be accepting of us, will they, though?' asked Aidan.

'I don't care about that. I care about you. I want to be with you – properly. People can throw insults my way all they want, as long as I've got you, Aidan.'

'Markus.' Aidan's heart hammered. Markus's face twitched the way it always did when he got nervous. They had never said it, though Markus had alluded to it so many times. Aidan wanted to make one thing very clear tonight. 'I love you.'

Markus's wide eyes and smile told Aidan his answer before the other young man's mouth was on his. They kissed for several minutes before Markus whispered back. 'I love you. I've been in love with you for many, many months.'

'I've been in love with you for many, many months too.'

Markus nibbled Aidan's lips. 'I love you, I love you, I love you,' he repeated quickly, peppering Aidan's face with kisses.

'God, I love you,' Aidan murmured. 'I was so drawn to you, didn't understand it until you kissed me, and I think I've been in love with you since.'

Markus's eyes glistened with tears. 'Aidan,' he whispered, tracing his fingers along his jawline, 'you have no idea how happy you make me – how happy you've made me to hear you say that.'

'Then let me tell you over and over again.' And Aidan repeated 'I love you' more times than Markus had. The two continued to make out and declare their love until it became too late to have any good excuse to be outside, and snuck back to their dorms.

* * *

The following morning.

Missus Turnabbey marched to Aidan, looking as scary and strict as always. He reflexively stood straighter.

'The Headmaster would like to speak with you immediately.'

Aidan felt a wave of fear. He followed in silence.

When he reached the Headmaster's office, Missus Turnabbey shut the door and locked it, leaving the two of them alone.

The Headmaster's face was stern, more than Aidan had ever seen him before. Aidan swallowed hard as his heart drummed anticipatedly.

'Do you know what the school policy is, lad?' the Headmaster seethed, his voice low and dangerous.

'Which policy in specific—'

'You know very well the one,' the Headmaster interrupted, voice raised.

'Uh...no dating, sir.' Aidan downcast his eyes, trying to focus on a spot in front of him.

'Yes. And what were you up to last night, young man?'

'I was not with any girl, sir.'

'Don't lie to me!' shouted the Headmaster. 'You were seen and heard declaring your love to someone.'

Aidan's stomach clenched. He let out a shaking breath and began to tremble.

'Who was she? How long has this been going on?'

Aidan could only stare, jaw clenched. 'I was with no one last night.' He wasn't going to get Markus into trouble too. He shut his eyes, hoping Markus would be all right.

'You defy me, boy?'

'Yes.' He would take whatever punishment the Headmaster threw his way. He expected expulsion, but he did not expect what came next.

'Shirt off.'

'Excuse me?'

The Headmaster reached behind his desk and produced a whip. Aidan drew in a sharp and shaking breath.

Aidan looked back at the locked door – it was guarded by Missus Turnabbey. Reflexively, he lifted his arm to shield himself, bringing a fist up to defend himself, but the Headmaster was strong, despite his age, and larger than the lad. The elder man twisted Aidan's arm back and kneed him in the stomach at the same time. Aidan cried out as pain shot up his arm, doubling over, and he was forced down onto his knees hard.

'Shirt off now. On your knees. It's time you were taught a lesson.'

* * *

Markus glanced at the empty seat beside him. Where the heck was Aidan? It wasn't like him to be late for class. Everyone was abuzz with whispers. Markus grew worried.

He leaned towards his classmate and asked, 'Have you seen Aidan since we left for breakfast?'

'Haven't you heard? Your best friend got called to the Headmaster's office.'

Markus scowled. 'What the heck for?'

'Someone overheard him declaring his love to someone last night.' Markus's heart sank as fear gripped him. 'And apparently, they were kissing too. I hear he's in for a good flogging.'

'No!' cried Markus. He was trembling. And before he knew what he was doing, he bolted out of class, tears already pouring down his face.

He raced towards the Headmaster's office and slammed face-first into Miss Mariane.

'Oof, Markus, watch where—' She stopped. 'What's happened?'

'It's Aidan. The Headmaster's going to flog him because last night' – he heaved – 'someone heard him declaring his love and kissing.'

'Oh, my.' Mariane put a hand to her mouth. The woman studied Markus. 'So he called him in because of the rule of not dating any of the girls—?'

'You don't understand, Miss Mariane, he wasn't *with* any girl last night.' Markus raked a hand through his hair. 'It's all my fault,' he whispered.

Mariane took a deep breath. 'Markus, whatever is going on, I want you to know it's safe to confide in me. I will not report you or anyone you mention. This stays between us. If I can help, I will.'

Markus somehow felt she was sincere. 'He was with me. I'm the one he declared his love to, and now he's being punished because we love each other.'

Mariane nodded, drawing in a breath as a sob escaped Markus. 'Right, come with me. We're going to get Aidan.'

Markus exhaled shakily, partly out of relief, partly out of fear. Mariane led him to the Headmaster's office, where Missus Turnabbey stood guard but stepped aside upon seeing Mariane, who used her key to barge in.

'Headmaster!' Mariane yelled.

Hand raised, the Headmaster paused and lowered his whip.

Kneeling in the centre of the room, his back bare, was Aidan. His back was striped red with whip marks, and there were faint smears of blood.

Markus reflexively ran to him, calling Aidan's name. He crouched before him, taking Aidan's face between his hands. Aidan's cheeks were streaked with tears.

'Markus.' Aidan's voice was hoarse as though he'd been screaming in pain.

'What is the meaning of this, Headmaster?' demanded Mariane.

'This lad has broken the rules and refuses to tell me who he was with last night.'

Markus's heart skipped a beat. 'You didn't tell him?' he whispered.

'I wanted to protect you.' Aidan's whisper was barely audible.

Markus was more in love with him now, but felt so guilty because he was the one whom he was with, because it was their love that had gotten him into trouble. Markus was just as guilty as Aidan was of breaking the rules.

Markus rose, meeting the Headmaster's stern gaze. With determined fire in his heart, he declared. 'I should be the one to be flogged.' He would take all the punishment for the young man he loved if he had to – he would not bear witness to Aidan being tormented anymore.

'Because they were rehearsing for an assignment I gave them,' Mariane cut in. 'They were together and practising the roles I had given them – love declarations. It seems they succeeded in their assignment before I could evaluate their sincerity. Acting must be believable, does it not?'

Markus nearly buckled to his knees. He mouthed a 'Thank you' while the Headmaster wasn't looking.

Markus helped Aidan to his feet and put his shirt back on him, his eyes pleading for forgiveness.

'This isn't your fault,' Aidan sorrowfully whispered.

'Is this the truth?' demanded the Headmaster.

'It is,' asserted Mariane.

'I hope so for your sake, Mariane, because if these lads were together and not on an assignment, that would be worse.'

Aidan winced, shutting his eyes tightly – Markus felt the sting as well.

The Headmaster left his office. Mariane walked up to the lads and took their hands in hers, leading them briskly to the dorms.

She pushed the dorm doors open and got their suitcases out. 'Pack. You must leave. It's no longer safe for the two of you here.'

'But where are we to go? We're not exactly at our homes' doorsteps,' protested Markus. Aidan hadn't uttered a word since they'd left the Headmaster's office.

'You'll go to my home. This should get you both on the train.' Mariane handed them a wad of money. 'Lilith will be able to take care of you until I can return home in a few days' time.'

'Lilith, your sister?' asked Markus.

Mariane averted her gaze for a brief second. 'She's…not my sister.' Markus understood.

Aidan was packing up. He looked up at Mariane. 'What about you? You'll get into trouble for this.'

'Whatever punishments await me are nothing compared to what you've already suffered. I'll deal with the Headmaster. Now, you two go before you're missed and he sends out a search party.'

Leading Aidan by the hand, Markus ran across the terrain.

Finally, out of breath, he slowed and let out a loud sob. 'I'm so sorry, Aidan.'

Aidan continued, giving no reply. Markus's chest clenched, he wanted to collapse then and there.

After walking for several more minutes, Aidan collapsed onto the ground, hand on his eyes and weeping. Markus stopped and turned to him. He knelt before him, weeping as well.

'Aidan, please say something to me.'

Aidan lifted his face, tears pouring from his eyes, mouth set in disdain. 'Markus, they can punish me how ever they like and throw all the flogs my way. I love you, and I don't think that will ever change.'

A sob escaped Markus's lips, the ache eased only a little.

Aidan reached a hand to Markus, his gentle caress filling him with relief, and Markus leaned his cheek into Aidan's touch. Aidan repeated in a whisper, 'I love you, and that will never change.'

* * *

Many months later — September 1980.

Aidan sat at the dinner table with Mariane and Lilith as Markus served the meal.

'It's wonderful to have you cooking for us, Markus,' voiced Mariane.

'It's the least I can do for all the two of you have done for us,' said Markus. He sat down beside Aidan.

'Now that the two of you have been settled for a bit, have you thought about what you're going to do next?'

'I think we owe one hell of an explanation to our parents,' said Aidan. 'Not sure how that's going to go, though.'

'One thing at a time, babe.' Markus smiled warmly.

'At least the Headmaster's been replaced,' said Lilith. 'I can't believe you didn't take the job, honey.'

'I reduced my days at the school,' said Mariane, 'I want to dedicate more time to you, love.'

'Aw,' both lads teased.

'And the new Headmaster's done much good already,' insisted Mariane. 'He introduced scheduled date nights for those who behave, which has been working surprisingly well. And he doesn't seem bothered by the prospect of any lads who might be interested in dating each other.'

She smiled in sympathy. 'Word, however, of your involvement together and what happened has spread. Most people agree that what you suffered was utterly reprehensible and an act of violence.'

The memory, while it sent a pang to Aidan's heart, no longer elicited a flashback of the physical pain he'd been in. Somehow, he knew his story would someday save others from suffering the same.

'You know,' began Aidan, his heart filled with hope, 'one day, people like the four of us, we're going to be accepted, and we're going to be able to get married.' He looked at Markus.

'Wouldn't that be nice,' said Markus.

'I'm telling you, it's going to happen. Markus, I love you – that's never going to change.'

'Same goes for me.'

'I want to marry you someday,' declared Aidan, feeling bold.

Markus's smile told him his answer before he voiced it. 'I'd love nothing more than to marry you and call you my husband, Aidan.'

* * *

Present day.

Aidan got down on one knee before Markus, whose face twitched nervously, in the adorable way it always did. 'So, let me ask you properly this time. Will you marry me?'

'Yes!' Markus laughed tearfully. 'So much, yes.'

Aidan let out a breath, also full of tears. 'I love you, Markus. I still love you, and that still will never change!'

'And the same still goes for me, Aidan.'

Laughing and weeping, the two middle-aged men kissed, and for the first time as they devoured each other breathlessly, they felt a joy they'd been waiting twenty-six years to feel.

<u>THANK YOU SO MUCH FOR READING</u>

If you enjoyed this story,
please consider taking a few moments
to write a review on Amazon or Goodreads.
It would mean so much.

Thank you.

Please enjoy this passage from

The Thief & His Hunter

BOOK 1

The first book in an ongoing series of
Dark Romance Thriller, Gay Romance books.

Warnings:
Strong language, violence.

CHAPTER 1

Conor took the photograph of the tiara from the siblings, studying it carefully. His hood covered most of his face, casting a shadow over most of his features, so he was careful when he looked up again to politely meet his clients' gazes without revealing *too* much of his face.

'Do you think you can retrieve it for us?' asked the young woman.

Conor nodded. 'This was stolen recently, yes? I think I can track it down easily.'

'That tiara was our grandmother's,' the brother offered. 'My sister has always been intent on wearing it to Prom.'

'When did it go missing?' asked Conor, placing the photo back on the table.

'Just last week. After the break-in.'

Conor thought about that. Most items he stole back for clients had been claimed long ago and sat in mansions or museums. This tiara either sat in a pawn-shop or in someone's home. Conor was no detective, but he had his ways of sniffing out anyone who was sus.

'I'll find it,' he assured.

'We filed a report with the Investigative Department of Police, but they wouldn't tell us what they found about any suspects.'

'Then I'll just have to break into the station.'

The brother gave Conor his payment – he always took half up-front. The young woman smiled at him.

'Maybe once you've found it, I can thank you properly.' She tucked a strand of hair behind her ear.

Conor chuckled, flattered. 'Sorry, but I'm gay. Not to mention far too old for you.' He reckoned he was at least a decade older.

Her brother stifled a laugh, nudging his sister.

Conor walked back to the window, glancing out. 'You never saw my face,' he declared, lifting his leg over the open window's railing.

'Hey, Vulpis?'

Conor paused and looked back at the siblings.

'Why did you choose that name for yourself?'

Conor grinned. 'Because I'm the sly fox.' He winked before leaping out of the window. He rolled to cushion his fall a storey and a half below.

He ran to the nearest apartment complex and scaled its fire escape stairs to the roof. He ran across the roof and leapt over the gap between the two blocks, the Autumn wind on his face, time almost stopping as the rush of the escape thrilled him. He landed in another roll. Then jumped down to a penthouse balcony, grabbed the railing, and swung out to the next roof, one storey lower. And off Conor bounded from roof to roof to his destination.

* * *

'What do you mean we got broken into? We're an investigative branch for the police, we've got security cameras all around the building. No one breaks into this place.' Theron slapped a hand to his forehead.

Martha stared back, looking amused. 'That's why I called you. Because the cameras caught a glimpse of our culprit.'

Sighing, Theron waved for his boss to go on and show him. She played the security footage on their high-tech screen. It showed a man leaping down the building from two stories higher. He was clad in black leather attire and wearing the signature hood of the very thief Theron had been hunting for years.

'Vulpis.' Theron paused the recording. 'That's why he got in undetected. Because he came during a time when few of us were here.' He pointed at the screen. 'No chance he turned around so we could see his face?'

'Vulpis is good. Never looks directly at the security cams.' Martha pointed at a corner of the screen. 'He used a slingshot to take out the adjacent camera.'

'A slingshot?' Theron shook his head in disbelief. 'I haven't heard of anyone using those since I was a kid.' He chuckled. 'Used to practise with my best friend all the time.'

'The one who got away?' asked Martha.

'Yeah. The one who moved away.' Theron strode out of the room. 'So what's our next step? How do we catch Vulpis? Feels like forever since I took over from Barry.' He shrugged. 'I'm never going to catch him at this rate.'

Martha followed as Theron grabbed his jacket and began towards the exit.

'There have to be witnesses to his crimes,' Theron went on. 'People who've seen his face.'

'No one talks. They all claim he helped them retrieve stolen goods.'

'Stolen goods?' Theron stopped, turning around. '*Vulpis* steals them. He breaks into museums, rich people's homes. He's breaking the law and getting on my nerves the longer I hunt him down to no avail.' Theron started off again. 'I can't wait to get my hands on him.'

* * *

Conor studied the layout of the house he was to steal from. The police report mentioned an identified suspect based on fingerprints. The burglar had taken the tiara to a pawnshop, as suspected. However, someone had already purchased the tiara and the shop owner ensured confidentiality of his clients.

The mansion had security cameras and guards patrolling the lavish gardens. Either this person was a successful businessperson or part of a mafia. Mobsters were easier to negotiate with if anything went wrong. Conor usually could offer to retrieve something for them and that sufficed. Anyone else, however, anyone who followed the law diligently, no negotiations possible.

Conor crept closer, keeping his hooded head below the bushes. He'd have to find a way around the guards. He wasn't trained to take them out. He was trained to scale, run, jump, and steal.

Finally, he saw his opening. He ran in a half-crouch across the terrain and jumped like a ballerina over the sprinklers, avoiding them. He pressed his back to the wall just as a guard rounded the corner. He turn-rolled, pressing himself to the bricks and slunk along to the large patio doors.

Lockpicking his way in, Conor tentatively slid the door open. So far so good. Aiming his slingshot, he sent a rock at the security camera in the corner of the room. It turned away from the door. Now Conor could creep along past here without being seen.

Grinning to himself, Conor left the patio door ajar before working his way to the side of the house. He jumped, latching onto a windowsill and pulled himself up. When he stood on the windowsill, he grabbed onto some of the jutting bricks and scaled his way to the roof.

He crept along the roof to an empty room's window. Grabbing the gutter, he dangled himself, slid his little stainless steel card-knife glass cutter along the side of the glass and sliced the window open with practised ease. He lowered himself just enough, angling his legs, and slunk into the dark room.

* * *

Martha marched to Theron. 'We've got a lead. Someone's tipped us off about a man, perhaps thirties, asking about a stolen tiara from a pawnshop owner. Matches the reports. We think he might be headed for whoever purchased this tiara.'

'Then it's time to crash the party.' Theron secured his gun, feeling a thrill. This was the first time in a long time they had a viable lead on Vulpis.

'Be careful,' Martha warned. 'We don't want to harm this guy. We want to take him in and question him. People praise him. And those of us hunting him . . .'

'Yeah, yeah, they're calling me the detective who's hounding him.' Theron became defensive. 'I never even met the guy. How am I supposed to be hounding a lawbreaker? A lawbreaker!'

'Just remember we want him alive.'

'Oh, I remember. I've been after this thief for so long, I *want* him alive, if only so he can answer all my questions.'

Theron gathered a small team and they left stealthily for the mansion where Vulpis was said to be.

* * *

Conor had the tiara. He wrapped it in a small shawl and stuffed it in his satchel. He was ready to make his way to his exit, and if he couldn't, he had that Plan B he'd secured earlier. There'd been no alarms. So far everything was going smoothly.

Conor paused. The corridor was quiet, but he heard something downstairs. A fast pitter-patter of shoes.

Conor cursed under his breath. The police were here – only *they* were this stealthy.

Conor veered the corner and entered the room he'd come in from. He peered out the window and saw officers sneaking along the perimeter. He couldn't exit from there.

Conor turned back and hurried to another room. It was an office of sorts – it would have to do. He ran to the window, peering out carefully.

Good, it seemed the officers were focused on his backup exit – that left this side of the house unguarded.

Conor lifted the window open, ready to jump out, when—

'Vulpis! Hands above your head.'

Conor paused as he heard the click of a gun. He stuck his head out the window. There was no easy access to the roof from here, nor to the ground, but there was a ladder just leaning against the wall – below it, paint cans. Conor couldn't believe his luck. He chuckled.

'I said hands above your head, thief.'

Aware of the gun aimed at his back, Conor slowly brought his hands up, preparing himself. If he could just bring the ladder closer. He reached an arm out, pulling on it. It teetered towards the window but got stuck on a jutting brick, still too far to help Conor down. *These fancy people and their fancy bricks.* These had served him moments before – not now.

The rush of footsteps alerted Conor to the officer squarely behind him – it was too late. The man pulled on Conor's hood, spinning him around to point his gun in his face.

Conor stared wide-eyed at the man who apprehended him. Taller than he remembered him, dark hair covering his thick brows, a thin goatee neatly trimmed around his luscious lips, his dark blue eyes vivid in contrast to the dim light that seemed to give his pastel skin a soft glow. And he was so much more handsome, it staggered Conor's heart.

'Theron?'

* * *

Theron gaped at the blond man before him, pale blue eyes just as earnest as he remembered them. He had a subtle hint of facial hair, far less pronounced than Theron's own, but enough to mark his years, and it made him all the more gorgeous.

'Conor?' Theron worked his jaw. 'You're . . . *you're* Vulpis?' Theron took a staggering step back. 'You're the thief I'm after?'

Conor grinned. 'So you're my hunter?'

Theron raked a hand through his hair, lowering his gun hand. He couldn't believe it. 'Damn, it's been . . . fifteen years.' He pressed his lips together. 'Fifteen years since you left.'

'Since *I* left?' Conor was defensive. 'I had no choice. My parents were moving – I *had* to follow them.'

'Across the country, several states away?'

'What was I supposed to do?' shrugged Conor. 'We were fifteen. Besides, it's not like my best friend was going to stop me because he decided to hate me.'

'I was angry, okay? You were abandoning me!'

Conor palm-clapped as he emphasised. 'I didn't abandon you. I had no choice but to follow my parents when we moved away.' He deflated. 'A mistake I learnt a year later when I . . .' He sighed.

Something clanked outside.

'Look, I *thought* you were abandoning me, okay?' Theron motioned towards the outside. 'You were leaving, so I decided to break up with my best friend because that was easier than dealing with abandonment.'

Conor's eyes reflected sadness, and it tugged at Theron's heart. 'I hadn't realised you felt that way.'

'Yeah, well.' Theron shrugged. 'Not that it matters now anyway.' He snapped himself back. 'We're grown-ups, and you're an infamous thief. I have been hunting you for many years. Now I get to identify who Vulpis is and track you down wherever you go.' Theron let out a soft chuckle. 'I guess apprehending you has turned into a catch-up.'

Conor grinned cheekily. 'Only if you can keep up and catch me.'

Conor leapt out of the window.

'Conor!'

Theron closed the distance to the window, reaching his arm out to grab Conor. And missing him. When he looked out, he couldn't see Conor, nor tell where or if he had landed safely.

Theron cursed under his breath. That taunt was exactly what Conor had told him the first time they'd met, when they were five. And Theron had caught him then – he would catch him now.

Theron ran back the way he'd come and down the stairs. He rushed out of the mansion, and saw movement in his periphery. He sprinted towards Conor who leapt over a short fence. Theron easily jumped over it, quickly catching up with the thief.

Conor reached the emergency stairs for an apartment building. Theron followed him up to the roof where Conor ran and jumped over the gap to the next roof.

Theron stopped on the edge of the roof, looking down, his heart pounding.

'You can do it.'

Theron was startled, realising Conor was staring at him from across the gap, arms crossed, a grin on the side of his mouth.

Theron motioned between them. 'What is this? You some sort of parkour expert now or something?'

'Actually, yes.' Conor approached the gap. 'Give yourself a running start, then leap like a ballerina when you jump.' Theron furrowed his brows, puzzled. 'Don't worry, Theron. I'll catch you. I won't let you fall.'

Theron merely gaped at him. Despite the situation, it was like no time had passed at all, almost like they had seen each other yesterday and were picking up where they had left off.

'You want to catch me, right? You want to have that catch-up?'

Theron pointed behind him. 'At the station!' Conor merely waited. 'You haven't changed one bit. You're just as reckless.' Theron rolled his eyes, clipping his gun to his belt. 'If I fall and break a limb . . .'

Conor reached a hand out towards him. 'I'll make sure you're safe.'

Theron felt crazy for considering this. He dreaded being high up, let alone on a roof like this. 'Fine.'

He backed away, took a deep breath, and then ran, leaping over the gap between the two buildings. Time stopped as the cool air whipped past his face.

His foot landed on the edge of the next rooftop. Conor grabbed Theron's hand, pulling him to him, and wrapped an arm around his waist, pressing him close to his body.

'I've got you.'

Theron had to look away, his head already feeling hot, aware that his face was nearly touching Conor's. Yet, the way the moon shone on Conor's face, emphasising the flush on his usually ivory cheeks, had Theron wanting to stare at him all night. It seemed like time had stopped, and a rush of heat threatened to make Theron forget himself.

Conor took a step back, leading Theron to the safety of the wide rooftop.

Theron stopped. He had so many questions. 'You could have tried to keep in touch,' he blurted.

Conor raised his brows. '*You* broke up with *me!* A harsh friendship break-up. I thought you hated me! It devastated me. It wasn't up to *me* to reach out to *you* after that. I was hurt.'

'Yeah, well, I was hurt too.'

Conor spread out his arms. 'Why didn't you just tell me that instead of acting like you hated me?'

'I don't know. It was easier, I guess. I thought you *wanted* to move away. I thought you wanted to leave me behind.'

'I was heartbroken about the move,' admitted Conor. 'Didn't know you felt just as heartbroken.'

'Yeah well, that's because . . .' Theron paused. His heart was beating so fast.

Theron and Conor stared at each other.

'I cried myself to sleep,' admitted Theron. It had wrenched his heart.

'Same.'

Then they spoke at the same time.

'Because I was in love with you.'

'Because I loved you.'

Eyes wide, both men dropped their jaws.

'You're gay too?' asked Conor, his surprise turning into a soft grin.

'Bi, actually,' said Theron. His breath hitched and he exhaled shakily. He averted his gaze.

Small hints of colour appeared on the horizon as the sun began to rise. Theron saw Conor's shadow approach as the thief took a step forward. He touched Theron's chin with his fingers, tilting it up slowly. Theron's heart skipped a beat.

Conor cupped Theron's face. 'And now? How do you feel seeing me after all these years? Because I can tell you right now, it doesn't matter how long it's been. I never stopped feeling things for you. And seeing you now is making me feel a lot more than I ever have before.'

Theron was trembling. He was nervous, and he was excited. 'It doesn't matter how I feel about you, Conor. We were teenagers. Maybe it might have worked out then, had we known, had we been able to admit it to each other. But I'm a detective, you're a thief.'

'I help people,' Conor insisted gently.

'You break the law.'

'*You* haven't changed one bit. Always such a stickler for rules.' Conor's tone was tender.

Theron downcast his eyes. 'We can't be together. How would it work?'

'I wasn't asking about the logistics of it. I was asking how you feel.'

Theron met Conor's gaze. 'Seeing you again . . . It's brought it all back. I knew it was you right away, as soon as I saw your face, and my heart leapt. It soared, and sank.' He paused. Conor waited. 'I still have feelings for you too. I think I always have, like you, continued to care even while pretending I had moved on with my life.'

Conor's smile was tender and it sent warmth to Theron's heart.

'Then we can figure this out, no? Now that we know how we feel about each other and how we felt back then too.'

Theron shook his head, and Conor removed his hand from Theron's face, his brows creasing with disappointment.

'I'm sorry. But I have to take you in, Conor.'

In one swift motion, Theron unclipped his gun and brought it up, holding it with both hands. 'Hands above your head, Vulpis. I need to take you in for questioning.'

Conor chuckled, backing away from Theron. Theron set his jaw. 'Conor, don't make this more difficult than it needs to be, *please*.'

'We'll talk again soon, I hope. We have a lot to unpack and resolve, it seems.' His smile turned into a grin. 'But you're worth it. Somehow, now that I know what that break-up was about, it says a lot about us. And meeting again . . .?'

'Conor?' Theron warned.

Conor merely grinned at him and winked. Then he fell back, hands grabbing onto the edge of the roof.

'Conor!' Theron screamed. He ran to him, peering down and barely catching sight of Conor slipping into an open window below.

Theron backed away from the edge of the roof, clutching his chest as he realised he feared more for Conor's safety than he was worried about catching him.

Breathing heavily, Theron waited to steady himself before making his way down.

Also By

Also Written by Eidahs

Sanguine Sincerity
(https://binkyproductions.com/supernaturalromance)

The Thief and His Hunter Book 1
The Thief and His Hunter Book 2
(https://binkyproductions.com/TheThiefandHisHunter)

Like Father, Not Like Sons
Legacy Takedown
Of Sullied Dreams and Beaten Hearts
Butchery At the Debauchery
Serendipitous Tribulation
Turbulent Justice
(https://binkyproductions.com/shortstories)

<u>Also Published by Binky Ink</u>

Stardust Destinies I: Variate Facing
Stardust Destinies II: The Drought
Stardust Destinies III: A Sublime Search
(https://binkyproductions.com/stardustdestinies)

The Hidden Cove: Pirate's Misadventure
(https://binkyproductions.com/shortstories)

About the Author

Eidahs is a pseudonym for all mature written works, from thrillers to erotic romance. Eidahs in pronunciation sounds elven in nature, which is why she chose it, to tap into her love of fantasy, a genre that couples well with super-natural and preternatural, dark fantasy, and romance.

Eidahs is also the nickname 'Shadie' backwards, repre-senting the shadow self, innermost desires, and a spectrum of emotions, most notably, passion, sorrow, rage, and delight, which Eidahs loves to incorporate in her writing. Enticing readers and evoking the characters' emotions when she writes has guided her inspiration to spell many short stories on Medium and a series of books under this pen name.

Connect with Binky Ink:

WordPress Website & Blog
   https://binkyproductions.com/binkyinkwriting
Medium – Main Profile
   https://medium.com/@BinkyInkWriting
X (Twitter) https://twitter.com/binkyinkwriting